THE BEST OF TAGORE

The Best of Tagore

Translated and compiled by
Jharna Basu

New York Toronto London Auckland
Sydney New Delhi Hong Kong

Published by Scholastic India Pvt. Ltd.
A subsidiary of Scholastic Inc., New York, 10012 (USA).
Publishers since 1920, with international operations in Canada, Australia,
New Zealand, the United Kingdom, India, and Hong Kong.

For information regarding permission, write to:
Scholastic India Pvt. Ltd.
A-27, Ground Floor, Bharti Sigma Centre
Infociti-1, Sector-34, Gurgaon 122001 (India)

First edition: June 2004
Reprinted: January 2014; November 2017, 2018, 2019, 2020

ISBN-13: 978-81-7655-333-9

Printed at Shivam Offset Press, New Delhi

Contents

Kabuliwala

My five-year old daughter Mini can't sit quiet even for a minute. She doesn't waste any time in silence. This irritates her mother greatly, and she would like to stop her prattle[1] for a while, but I would not. Being quiet is unnatural for Mini, and I cannot bear her silence for long either. My own chats with her are always fun.

One morning, as I was in the midst of the 17th chapter of my new novel, my little Mini tiptoed into the room, and putting her hand on mine, said: "Father! Ramdayal, our guard, calls a crow a *kauwa*! He doesn't know anything, does he?"

Before I could explain to her the difference between one language and another she hopped over to another subject. "Is it true, Father? Bhola says that there is an elephant in the clouds blowing water out of his trunk, and that is why it rains. It's rubbish, isn't it?"

And then, darting[2] off anew, while I sat still, trying to think of some reply to this: "Father! What relation is mother to you?"

You little wretch! I said to myself. But pulling a long face I managed to say: "Go and play with Bhola, Mini! I am working!"

The window of my room overlooks the road. The child had seated herself at my feet near the table, and started chanting softly, drumming her fingers on her knees. I was hard at work[3] on my 17th chapter, in which Pratap Singh, the gallant hero,

1 Chatter
2 Moving quickly and suddenly
3 Busy with work

has just caught Kanchanlata, the heroine, in his arms, and is about to jump with her by the third-storey window, of the castle, when suddenly Mini left her game, and ran to the window, crying—"A Kabuliwala! A Kabuliwala!" and indeed, in the street below, there was a Kabuliwala, walking slowly along. He wore a loose, soiled robe and a high turban; he carried a bag on his back, and boxes of grapes in his hand.

I cannot tell what my daughter's feelings were when she saw this man, but she began calling him loudly. *Ah!* I thought; *Now he will come in, and my 17th chapter will never get finished!* At that very moment the Kabuliwala turned, and looked up at the child. When she saw him coming, she got scared, and ran to her mother's protection. She had a fear that inside the bag, which the big man carried, there were perhaps two or three children like herself. Kabuliwala, meanwhile, entered my gate and greeted me with a smile.

Though my hero and my heroine were in such a precarious[4] condition, I thought I should buy something, since Mini had called the man to the house. I bought a few things, and we began to talk about Abdur Rahman, the Russians, the English, and the Frontier policy.

As he was about to leave, he asked: "And where is your little girl, sir?"

And then, thinking that Mini must get over her fear, I had her brought out.

She stood by my chair, and stared suspiciously at the Kabuliwala and his bag. He offered her nuts and raisins, but Mini perhaps feeling shy, just stood clinging to me, with all her fears unchanged.

4 Uncertain, depending on chance

This was their first meeting!

A few mornings later, however, as I was leaving the house, I was startled to find Mini, seated on a bench near the door, laughing and talking, with the great Kabuliwala at her feet. In her five-year-old life, it appeared, my small daughter had never found so patient a listener, except her father. And already the corner of her little sāri was stuffed with almonds and raisins, a gift from her visitor.

"Why did you give her those?" I said, and taking out an eight-anna coin, I handed it to him. The man accepted the money quietly, and put it into his bag.

Only on my return, an hour later, I found the coin had made twice its own worth of trouble! For the Kabuliwala had given it to Mini: and her mother, catching sight of [5] it, had pounced on the child with "Where did you get that eight-anna coin?"

"The Kabuliwala gave it to me," announced Mini cheerfully.

"The Kabuliwala gave it you!" cried her mother. "Oh Mini! How could you take it from him?"

Mini's lips started trembling, "I didn't take it, he gave it to me himself."

I had entered just in time to save her from her mother's questioning. But I had my own queries.

It was not the first or the second time, I found, that the two had met. The Kabuliwala had overcome the child's terror by winning her over with gifts of nuts and almonds, and the two were now the best of friends.

They had many oft-repeated jokes, which amused them greatly. Mini would seat herself before him, look down on his

---

5 Getting a glimpse of

gigantic[6] frame in all her tiny dignity, and her face rippling with laughter would begin:

"Kabuliwala! What have you got in your bag?"

And he would reply, in the nasal accents of a mountaineer – "An elephant!"

And how they both enjoyed the joke! As for me, I quite enjoyed this grown-up man's laughter along a young child's.

Then the Kabuliwala, not to be left behind would take his turn: "Well, little one, when will you go to your in-laws' house?"

Now, nearly every small Bengali girl had heard long ago about her father-in-law's house; but we were the new generation, and had kept these things from our child, so that Mini couldn't fully understand this question. But she would not show it, and would counter-question, "Are you going there?"

Amongst men of the Kabuliwala's class, however, it is well known that the word 'in-law's house' has a double meaning. It is a euphemism[7] for jail, the place where we are well cared for, at no expense to ourselves. In this sense would the sturdy peddler[8] take my daughter's question. "Oh," he would say, shaking his fist at an invisible policeman, "I will thrash my father-in-law!" Hearing this, and picturing the poor father-in-law, Mini would go off into peals of laughter.

Mini's mother is very timid. So, she was full of doubts about the Kabuliwala, and advised me to keep a watchful eye on him.

If I tried to laugh her fear gently away, she would turn round seriously, and ask me solemn[9] questions like: "Are children

---

6 Huge
7 A mild inoffensive word or phrase used in place of one that is harsh, blunt or offensive
8 Seller of small articles
9 Serious

never kidnapped?", "Is it not true that there was slavery in Kabul?", "Is it so very impossible for this big man to carry off a tiny child?"

I urged that, though not impossible, it was very improbable. But this was not enough, and her fear persisted. But as it was a very vague fear, it did not seem right to forbid the man coming to our house, and the intimacy went on unchecked.

Once a year, in the middle of January, Rahman, the Kabuliwala, returned to his own country, and as the time approached, he would be very busy, going from house to house collecting his debts. This year, however, he would always find time to come and see Mini. It might have seemed to a stranger that there was some conspiracy[10] between the two, for when he could not come in the morning, he showed up in the evening.

Even to me it was a little startling now and then, suddenly to see this tall, loose-garmented man laden with his bags, in the corner of a dark room. But when Mini ran in smiling, with her "Kabuliwala! Kabuliwala!" and the two friends, so far apart in age, melted into their old laughter and their old jokes, my heart swelled.

One morning, I was correcting proofs[11] in my study—this was a few days before he had made his travel plans. It was chilly. Through the window, the rays of the sun touched my feet, and the light warmth was very welcome. It was nearly eight o'clock, and early pedestrians were up and about, their heads covered.

Suddenly, I heard an uproar in the street, and, looking out saw Rahman being led away bound between two guards and behind them a crowd of inquisitive[12] boys. There were bloodstains on

10 Grouping together for a secret purpose
11 A trial copy of printed material so that corrections can be made
12 Eager to know

his clothes, and one of the guards carried a bloodstained knife. I hurried out, and stopping them, enquired what it all meant. Partly from one, partly from another, I gathered that a certain neighbour had owed the peddler something for a Rampuri shawl, but had later denied buying it, and that in the course of the quarrel, Rahman had struck him.

Now, in his excitement, the prisoner began calling his enemy all sorts of names, when suddenly in a verandah of my house appeared my little Mini, with her usual call: "Kabuliwala! Kabuliwala!"

Rahman's face lighted up as he turned to her. He had no bag under his arm today, she could not talk about the elephant with him. So she promptly jumped to the next question, "Are you going to your in-law's house?"

Rahman laughed said, "That is just where I am going, little one!" Then seeing that the reply did not amuse the child, he held up his fettered[13] hands. "Ah!" he said, "I would have thrashed that old father-in-law, but my hands are bound!"

On a charge of murderous assault, Rahman was sentenced to a few years' imprisonment.

Time passed, and he was forgotten. Our usual life went on, and the thought of the once free mountaineer spending his years in prison seldom came to us. Even my fickle-hearted[14] Mini, I am embarrassed to admit, soon forgot her old friend. New friends filled her life. As she grew older, she spent more time with girls. Now she hardly came to her father's room, and I had much less opportunity of speaking to her.

Years flew by. It was once more autumn, and we had made arrangements for our Mini's marriage. It was to take place

---

13 Chained
14 Changing easily

during the Puja holidays. With Durga returning to Kailash, the light of our home would also leave for her husband's house.

It was a bright morning. After the rains, it seemed as though the air had been washed clean and the rays of the sun looked like pure gold. So bright were the rays that they made even the discoloured brick walls of Kolkata lanes look radiant. Since dawn the wedding pipes had been playing, and at each burst of sound my own heart throbbed[15] in pain. The soulful tunes of Bhairavi, seemed to intensify the dull ache I felt at the approaching separation. My Mini was to be married that evening.

From early morning, noise and bustle filled the house. In the courtyard, there was the canopy[16] to be put on the bamboo poles; there were chandeliers with tinkling sounds waiting to be hung in each room and verandah. There was no end of hurried movements and excitement. I was sitting in my study, looking through the accounts, when someone entered, saluted respectfully, and stood before me. It was Rahman, the Kabuliwala. At first I did not recognise him. He carried no bag, his long hair was cut short and his old vigour seemed to have gone. But finally he smiled, and I recognised him at once.

"When did you come, Rahman?" I asked him.

"Last evening," he said, "I was released from jail."

The words struck harshly upon my ears. I had never before talked to a criminal and my heart shrank within itself when I realised this; I couldn't help feeling that it would be better if he left soon on this auspicious day.

"There are ceremonies going on," I said, "and I am busy. Perhaps you could come another day?"

15 Beat strongly and regularly
16 A roof-like covering

He immediately turned to go; but as he reached the door he hesitated, and said, "May I not see the little one, sir, for a moment?"

He perhaps thought that Mini was still the same. He had pictured her running to him as she used to, calling "Kabuliwala! Kabuliwala!" He had imagined, too, that they would laugh and talk together, just as of old. Indeed, in memory of[17] former days, he had brought, carefully wrapped up in a paper, a few almonds and raisins and grapes, obtained somehow maybe, from a friend; he didn't have his own bag that day.

I repeated, "There is a ceremony in the house, and you will not be able to see anyone today."

The man's face fell. He looked wistfully[18] at me for a moment, then said "Good morning," and went out.

I felt a little sorry, and would have called him back, but I found he was returning himself. He came close up to me and held out his offerings, "I have brought these, sir, for the little one. Will you give these to her?"

I took them, and was going to pay him, but he caught my hand and said, "You are very kind, sir! I'll always remember you. Do not offer me money! You have a little girl... I too have one like her in my own home. I think of her, and bring this fruit for your child—not to earn for myself."

Saying this, he put his hand inside his big loose robe, and brought out a small and dirty piece of paper. Unfolding it with great care, he smoothed it out with both hands on my table. It bore the impression of a little hand. Not a photograph. Not a painting. Merely the impression of an ink-smeared hand laid flat on the paper. This touch of the hand of his own little daughter

17 In remembrance of
18 Thoughtfully and sadly

he had carried always next to his heart, as he had come year after year to Kolkata to sell his wares in the streets. Tears welled up in my eyes. I forgot that he was a poor Kabuli fruit seller, while I was a well-to-do respectable gentleman. I understood in that moment that he and I were the same, he was a father of a young daughter and so was I.

That impression of the hand of his little daughter in her distant mountain home reminded me of my own little Mini.

I sent for Mini immediately. Some objections were raised, but I swept them aside. Clad in the red silk saree of her wedding day, with the sandalwood paste on her forehead, and dressed up as a young bride, Mini came and stood shyly beside me.

The Kabuliwala seemed amazed at the change. He could not revive[19] their old friendship. At last he smiled and said, "Little one, are you going to your father-in-law's house?"

But Mini now understands the meaning of the word 'father-in-law' very well, and she could not answer him as of old. She blushed at the question, and turned away.

I remembered the day when the Kabuliwala and my Mini had first met, and I felt sad. When she had gone, Rahman sighed deeply and sat down on the floor. He had suddenly realised that his daughter too must have grown up, while he had been away so long, and that he would have to reintroduce himself to her too. Assuredly he would not find her as she was when he saw her last. What all could have happened to her in these eight years?

The marriage pipes sounded, and the mild autumn sunlight streamed round us. Rahman sat in the little Kolkata lane, but was lost in the bare mountains of Afghanistan.

---

19 To bring back

I took out a currency note, gave it to him, and said: "Go back to your daughter, Rahman, to your own country, and may the happiness of your reunion bring good fortune to my child!"

Having made this present, I had to cut down on some other festivities. I could not have the electric lights I had wanted, nor the military band, and the young girls of the house were a little upset about it. But to me the wedding-feast was all the more brighter with the thought that in a distant land a long-lost father would meet his only child again.

The Parrot's Training

Once upon a time there was a bird. It was ignorant. It sang all right, but had no clue about scriptures[20]. It hopped prettily around, but sadly lacked in manners.

The king thought, *Ignorance proves costly in the long run. For fools eat as much food as their betters, and yet give nothing in return.* He called his nephews for a meeting and told them that the bird *must* get sound schooling.

The pundits were summoned, and at once they went to the root of the matter. They decided that the ignorance of birds was due to their natural habit of living in lowly nests. Therefore, the first thing necessary for this bird's education was a suitable cage.

The pundits got their rewards and went home happy.

A golden cage was built with elaborate decorations. Crowds came to see it from all over the world.

"Culture, captured and caged!" exclaimed some, and in a rapture of ecstasy, burst into tears.

Others remarked: "Even if culture be missed, the cage will remain, to the end, a substantial fact. How fortunate for the bird!"

The goldsmith filled his bag with money and lost no time in sailing homewards.

The pundit sat down to educate the bird. With proper deliberation he took his pinch of snuff, as he said: "Textbooks

can never be too many for our purpose!"

The nephews brought together an enormous crowd of scribes[21]. They copied from books, and copied from copies, till the manuscripts piled up... to an unreachable height!!

People murmured in amazement: "Oh, the tower of culture, impressively high! Its end is lost in the clouds!"

The scribes, with light hearts and heavy pockets hurried home.

The nephews were furiously busy, keeping the cage spick and span.

As their constant scrubbing and polishing went on, the people said with satisfaction, "This is progress indeed."

Men were employed in large numbers, and supervisors even more. These, with their cousins of all different degrees of distance, built a palace for themselves and lived there happily ever after.

Whatever may be its other deficiencies, the world is never short of fault-finders; and they went about saying that everyone remotely connected with the cage flourished beyond words, except the bird.

When this remark reached the king's ears, he summoned his nephews before him and said: "My dear nephews, what is this that we hear?"

The nephews said, "Sir, let the testimony of the goldsmiths and the pundits, the scribes and the supervisors, be taken, if the truth is to be known. The fault-finders are so hawkish[22] because they are jealous!"

---

21 Persons who wrote out documents, especially before printing was invented (historical)
22 Like a hawk

The king found their explanation so luminously satisfactory that he presented each one of them with his own rare jewels.

One day, the king, desirous of seeing for himself how his Education Department handled the little bird, made an appearance at the great Hall of Learning.

From the gate rose the sound of conch shells and gongs, horns, bugles and trumpets, cymbals, drums and kettledrums, tambourines, flutes, fifes, barrel organs and bagpipes. The pundits began chanting mantras at the top of their voices, while the goldsmiths, scribes, supervisors, and their numberless cousins of all different degrees of distance, raised a round of cheers.

The nephews smiled and said: "Sir, what do you think of it all?"

The king said: "It does seem so fearfully like a sound Principle of Education!"

Mightily pleased, the king was about to remount his elephant, when the fault-finder, from behind a bush, cried out: "Maharaja, have you seen the bird?"

"Indeed, I have not!" exclaimed the king. "I completely forgot about the bird."

Turning back, he asked the pundits about the method they followed in instructing the bird.

It was shown to him. He was suitably impressed. The method was so pompous[23] that the bird looked ridiculously unimportant in comparison. The king was satisfied that there was no flaw in the arrangements. As for any complaint from the bird itself, that simply could not be expected. Its throat was so completely choked with the pages from the books that it could neither whistle nor whisper. It was thrilling just to watch the process.

---

23 In a grand fashion

This time, while mounting his elephant, the king ordered his State Ear-Puller to give a thorough good pull at both the ears of the fault-finder.

The bird thus crawled on, duly and properly, to the safest verge of inanity. In fact, its progress was satisfactory to the extreme. Nevertheless, nature occasionally triumphed over training, and when the morning light peeped into the bird's cage it sometimes fluttered its wings in a funny way. And, though it is hard to believe, it pitifully pecked at its bars with its feeble beak.

"What impudence[24]!" growled the guard.

The blacksmith, with his forge and hammer took his place in the king's Department of Education. Oh, what a resounding blow! The iron chain was soon completed, and the bird's wings were clipped.

The king's nephews looked black, and shook their heads, saying: "These birds not only lack good sense, but also gratitude!"

With textbook in one hand and the rod in the other, the pundits gave the poor bird what may rightly be called lessons!

The guard was honoured with a title for his watchfulness, and the blacksmith for his skill in forging chains.

The bird died.

Nobody had any idea when did it happen! The fault-finder was the first man to spread the rumour[25].

The king called his nephews and asked them: "My dear nephews, what is this that we hear?"

The nephews said: "Sir, the bird's education has been completed."

"Does it hop?" the king enquired.

---

24 Disrespect
25 Gossip; a report in circulation which is not necessarily true

"Never!" said the nephews.

"Does it fly?"

"No."

"Bring me the bird," said the king.

The bird was brought to him, guarded by the guards and the horsemen. The king poked its body with his finger. Only its inner stuffing of book-leaves rustled.

Outside the window, the murmur of the spring breeze amongst the newly budded Ashoka leaves made the April morning wistful.

The Rat's Feast

"It's so unfair!" said the boys. "We refuse to study under the new teacher."

The new Sanskrit teacher who was coming was called Kalikumar Tarkalankar.

The vacation was over and the boys were returning to school by train. A naughty boy had already changed the name of the teacher and made up a rhyme called *The Sacrifice of the Black Pumpkin* which they were repeating aloud in chorus.

At Adkhola station an elderly gentlemen boarded the train. He had with him a bedroll, two or three earthen pots, their tops covered with cloth, a tin trunk and a few bundles. A rowdy boy, whom everyone called Bichkun shouted at him, "No room here, Mr Dundle Head, go to another compartment."

The old man said, "The whole train is packed[26], there's no room anywhere. I'll sit in this corner and won't trouble you at all." He vacated the seat, rolled out his bed in one corner and settled down.

Then he asked the boys, "Where are you going, children, and for what?"

Bichkun retorted[27], "To perform last rites."

"Whose last rites?" asked the old man.

"Black Pumpkin Fresh Chilli," came the reply, and the boys

---

26 Full
27 Replied quickly

started chanting the rhyme.

The train pulled up at Asansol and the old man got down briefly to have a bath. When he returned, Bichkun said, "It'll be better if you move out of this compartment, Sir."

"Why?"

"There're rats all over..."

"Rats? Don't tell me!"

"See what they've done to your pots."

The old gentlemen saw that all the sweets in the two pots had been polished off[28].

"They also ran off with whatever you had in that bundle of yours." The bundle had a few ripe, mangoes.

The old gentlemen smiled and said, "Poor rats! They must have been famished[29]."

"Oh no," said Bichkun, "They are like that. They eat even if they're not hungry."

The boys roared with laughter and said, "If there had been more, they'd have devoured[30] that too."

The gentleman said, "It's all my fault. If I'd known there would be so many rats on the train, I'd have brought more."

Despite all these pranks, seeing that the old man was not angry, the boys were rather disappointed. It would have been fun to see him lose his temper.

At Bardhaman the train was to stop for an hour. They had to change the train. The old gentleman said, "I won't trouble you any more. I can find a seat in another compartment of this train."

"Oh no. You'll travel with us. If there's anything left in your

---

28 Finished quickly
29 Very hungry
30 To eat greedily

bundle, we'll watch it together and nothing will go missing."

The gentleman said, "All right, boys. You get on the train, I'll come in a minute."

They got on the train. In a short while a sweet vendor, accompanied by the old man, came to their window pushing his cart. He handed everyone a packet of sweets, saying, "This time the rats won't go hungry."

The boys let out a hurrah and started jumping about. The mango-seller came along with his basket of mangoes which were added to the feast.

The boys said to the gentleman, "Tell us where you are going and to do what...?"

"I'm on the look out for a job," said he. "I'll get off wherever I find a suitable one."

They asked, "What do you do?"

He said, "I'm a Sanskrit teacher."

They all clapped and said, "In that case, it will be great to have you in our school."

"Why would the management[31] engage me?"

"They'll have to! We won't let Black Pumpkin Fresh Chilli set foot-in the neighbourhood."

"You're making things hard for me. What, if the Secretary doesn't like me?"

"He'll have to—or else, all of us will leave the school."

"Very well. My boys, take me to your school."

The train arrived at the station. The Secretary himself was waiting. Seeing the old gentleman, he said, "Welcome Sir, Mr Tarkalankar! Your rooms are ready."

And he bent down to touch his feet.

---

31 Group of people running the school

Atonement

Manindra was about fourteen years old. He was very intelligent but not very industrious. Still he got through the annual examinations because of his natural intelligence. He did not live up to the expectations of his teachers. Manindra's father Divyendu was the principal of the school. His son's laziness and indifference worried him.

Akshay was in the same class as Manindra. He was poor and banked on scholarships. His widowed mother took great pains in bringing him up. When his father Priyanath was alive, he earned well, and was highly respected, but he spent his money freely. When he died, it became apparent that his savings would not pay off even half of what he owed. Akshay's mother Savitri sold all her jewellery and household goods and gradually paid off her deceased husband's debts.

Savitri was a skilled craftswoman. She made money by doing silk and zari embroidery on cloth and knitting socks and vests on a machine. For this she worked day and night and sometimes spent sleepless nights working.

Savitri's husband had a friend called Sanjay Moitra. Once Priyanath had borrowed a hefty sum and bailed him out. Sanjay had not forgotten the good turn and after Priyanath's death he repeatedly offered to help financially. But Savitri turned down the offer. She did not believe in living on charity.

Savitri was once invited to attend the thread ceremony of

Sanjay's son. When she arrived with Akshay by a cheap hired carriage, no one took any notice of her.

That day Savitri had to get back early. The tailor was to come to collect an embroidered piece by three o'clock in the afternoon. She requested Sanjay's wife Nrityakali to allow them to eat early so that they could leave.

Nrityakali was haughty and didn't care one way or the other about Savitri's request. She was busy getting food ready for her rich relations and did not consider Savitri fit to sit with them for a meal.

Savitri pleaded with the maid of the house to get her a hired carriage so that she could go home.

"I'll see," said the maid nonchalantly but did nothing!

Akshay was very young then. He said he would go and call the carriage.

Savitri asked him not to. She walked home with Akshay, gave him some puffed rice to eat and ate nothing herself. That was the first day Akshay had seen his mother in tears. It was then that he had pledged himself to removing his mother's distress and dishonour. He studied day and night and passed yearly examinations with flying colours.

Akshay came first, always. Manindra was more intelligent but could never surpass him in examinations.

This year, too, the examination came around. Manindra did quite well in all subjects except mathematics in which the questions seemed tough.

Akshay was writing his paper sitting next to Manindra. The lunch break was at one o'clock. Akshay finished his paper and left before one o'clock, leaving his answer sheets on the desk. Manindra lifted two sheets without anyone noticing.

Akshay did not do well. He had expected a scholarship,

so everyone was surprised when he did not get one. This time Manindra received it. His father Divyendu was the one to be surprised most. He couldn't understand how it could have happened. One day, suddenly the truth dawned on him. In the drawer of Manindra's study table he discovered two answer sheets in Akshay's handwriting. Manindra owned up his cheating.

On the day of the prize distribution Manindra's name was announced for the first prize. With the award in his hand he said, "I'm not entitled to this award. This is Akshay's by right. I've done wrong."

On reaching home Divyendu said to Manindra, "This is not the end! You've not yet made amends for the wrong you did. You'll have to pay Akshay's monthly stipend of fifteen rupees."

Manindra didn't know how he could do that. Divyendu said, "For one year you'll walk to school. The amount spent on your transport will pay for Akshay's stipend."

The Nuisance

Sharat and his wife Kiranmoyi sat chatting in a closed room in a garden house in Chandannagar one stormy evening. Kiranmoyi had been very ill. Everyone in her family and neighbourhood, even her mother-in-law, was fond of Kiran. So when the doctor suggested a change of place, no one raised any objection. Sharat had taken the Chandannagar house and brought Kiranmoyi there to recover. Kiran was making good progress, but felt lonely and bored because she had no friends and nothing to do except live the life of an invalid.

On this stormy evening Sharat was saying to Kiran, "If you stay here a little longer, you'll make full recovery."

Kiran said, "I'm fine now. Going home will not harm me in any way." While they were arguing on this, a servant called from outside.

Sharat opened the door and was informed that a Brahmin boy, whose boat had sunk, had swum ashore and walked into their garden. Immediately Kiran took out some dry clothes from the rack, heated a glass of milk and asked for the Brahmin boy to be brought to the inner room.

The boy had longish hair, large eyes and not even the slightest sign of any hair growth on his upper lip. Kiran herself supervised his meal and enquired about him. It turned out that he belonged to a troupe of strolling players and his name was

Nilkanta. The troupe was hired to perform at the nearby Sinha household. They were on their way when the boat sank. He did not know what happened to the others. He was a good swimmer and had somehow managed to save his own life.

The boy stayed on. The fact that he had a narrow escape[32] aroused Kiran's compassion[33].

Sharat was relieved to think that Kiran had now found a new interest which would keep her in Chandannagar for a while. And Nilkanta on his part was pleased with his transfer from the clutches of his manager and death, to this prosperous family.

But before long Sharat changed his mind and wanted to get rid of Nilkanta. Nilkanta had begun to smoke Sharat's hookah secretly. On rainy days, he took Sharat's favourite silk umbrella nonchalantly to roam around the village to make new friends. He spoilt a stray dog to such an extent that it entered Sharat's well-decorated room and soiled the spotless bedspread. Soon he had acquired a devoted following of children around himself and that year the green mangoes of the village mango grove got no chance to ripen.

Kiran did pamper the boy too much. She would dress him up in Sharat's discarded clothes, call him every now and then to amuse herself. He would act out a mythological story with dramatic gestures. Thus the long afternoon passed very quickly. Kiran tried to get Sharat to join in as well but he was invariably irritated. Nilkanta's talent did not blossom in his presence either.

Nilkanta often got whacks and scoldings from Sharat, but these did not bother him much as he was used to harsher treatment. He took it for granted that human existence was divided between pleasure and pain and that there was more

32 Barely escaping danger
33 A feeling of sympathy

pain than pleasure.

It was difficult to know Nilkanta's precise age. He had joined the theatrical group when he was very young and played the roles of mythological heroines such as Sita and Radha! Now he looked like an immature 17-year-old with his lack of facial hair and his simple, innocent eyes.

As he continued to stay at Sharat's house, he suddenly started feeling like a 17-year-old young man and if Kiran asked him to dress up as a girl for fun, he would just disappear. As these changes were taking place within Nilkanta, Sharat's brother Satish arrived from Kolkata to spend his college vacation in the garden house.

Kiran was delighted to receive him. He was the same age as her. All day long the two of them amused themselves playing tricks on each other. Sometimes she wrote 'monkey' on the back of his shirt and sometimes she locked him in. Satish did not take all this lying down either. He took his revenge by stealing her keys, putting chilli in her paan and tying the end of her sari to the foot of the bed while she was not looking. They spent the days chasing each other, sometimes fighting and then asking for forgiveness and making peace.

Nilkanta started behaving as though he was possessed[34]. He looked for excuses to quarrel. He was full of bitterness. He reduced his devoted followers to tears, kicked his pet stray dog for no reason so that its whines filled the air and he savagely hit the plants along the path as he went about the village.

Kiran was fond of feeding people who enjoyed eating. Nilkanta loved eating and Kiran took pleasure in calling and

---

34 To be dominated or controlled by

feeding him under her personal supervision. After Satish's arrival on the scene, Kiran was sometimes absent when Nilkanta came to eat. Previously he did not mind and would finish his food with the same satisfaction. But now if Kiran did not call him herself, he would lose his appetite and say to the maid in a voice choked with tears, "I'm not hungry."

Nilkanta was convinced that Satish maligned[35] him to Kiran. Lying on his bed, listening to the two poking fun at each other and laughing, he would have liked to use his Brahminical powers to turn Satish to ashes.

Nilkanta did not have the courage to harm Satish openly, but he took great pleasure in doing things to trouble him. One day Kiran asked Nilkanta to entertain Satish with one of his favourite songs, but Nilkanta did not Respond. Surprised, Kiran said, "What's the matter?"

"I've forgotten it," Nilkanta replied and went out.

At last it was time to leave. Everyone started packing, but it did not occur to anyone to tell Nilkanta about this. Kiran wanted to take Nilkanta with them, but she was outvoted. Finally, two days before their departure, she kindly suggested to Nilkanta that he return to his native place. After so many days of neglect, these kind words were too much for him to bear and he burst into tears. Kiran felt guilty, but Satish was merciless. He told his sister-in-law that Nilkanta had no reasons to cry. He had been treated like a king and knowing that he had to return to his former position, he was shedding crocodile tears[36].

Nilkanta was mortified[37] and would have killed Satish if he could.

---

35 Defamed
36 Fake tears; insincere sorrow
37 Humiliated

Satish had bought an ornamental inkstand in Kolkata. He was very attached to it and took great care in cleaning and polishing it, often with a silk handkerchief.

On the morning before their departure, the inkstand went missing. Satish was livid[38] and accused Nilkanta of stealing it, in the presence of Kiran. Nilkanta had swallowed many insults from Satish until now. But this time one more word from Satish would have made Nilkanta pounce on him like an angry kitten.

Kiran took Nilkanta to the next room and said gently, "if you have taken the inkstand, give it to me. No one need know anything about it." Tears welled up in his eyes and he started crying.

Kiran came out and said, "I'm certain Nilkanta hasn't stolen the inkstand."

Both Sharat and Satish refused to accept this, but could do nothing for fear of incurring Kiran's displeasure.

Kiran was deeply affected by the incident. She wanted to make amends. In the evening she went quietly to Nilkanta's room with a few items of clothing and a ten-rupee note. She wanted to slip these tokens of affection into his trunk which was also a gift from her.

She opened the trunk but could not put the gifts inside as it had been filled with a spool of kite string, polished shells and similar items. She thought of rearranging the items and started to empty it. At the bottom of the trunk was the missing inkstand.

Kiran sat there brooding for a long time with the inkstand in her hand. Unknown to her, Nilkanta had come into the room. He saw everything. He thought, Kiran herself had come secretly

38 Very angry

to catch him and he had been caught red-handed. How could he explain that he was not an ordinary thief? He had done this to take revenge and was going to throw it into the river. He had stolen it and yet he was not a thief. He could neither prove his innocence nor could he bear the thought of being taken for a thief by Kiran. Kiran heaved a deep sigh and replaced all the items with her gifts on top.

But the next day no one could find the boy. "Let's now search his trunk," said Sharat.

"You'll do no such thing," said Kiran adamantly. She had the trunk brought to her room, took out the inkstand and threw it into the river while no one was watching.

Within a day Sharat left the garden house with his family and the house had a deserted air. Only Nilkanta's pet stray dog refused to eat and went around searching for his master on the riverbank, howling continually.

Wish Fulfilment

Subalchandra's son was called Sushilchandra. But a name does not always reflect the person. 'Subal' means 'strong' but he was rather frail[39] and 'Sushil' means well-behaved but he was not really that!

Sushil troubled the whole neighbourhood with his pranks. His father could not always get hold of him to straighten him up because the boy was nimble while the father's rheumatism had made him slow.

It was a Saturday and the school closed early, but Sushil did not want to go to school because there was a class test. More than that, he wanted to spend the whole day preparing for a firework display in the evening.

When it was time to go to school, he told his father that he had a tummy ache and could not go. Subal knew how to cure the boy's 'tummy ache'. So he said, "In that case, you can stay at home. Hari will go to watch the firework. Pity, I'd got some toffees for you, but you can't have them now. Instead, I'll get you some of that bitter medicine. Just lie down there and I'll prepare the medicine." Saying this, he locked the boy in and went off.

Now Sushil was in a quandary[40]. He hated the medicine as

---

39 In poor health
40 Uncertainty

much as he loved the toffees. Even the firework display was denied to him.

When Sushil's father returned with the cup of medicine he sprang up and declared, "I'm all right now. I think I'll go to school." His father forced the boy to gulp down the medicine, advised him to rest, locked the room and left.

Sushil cried all day and thought to himself, *If I were as old as my father, I could do as I pleased and no one could lock me up.*

Sushil's father Subal sat outside alone thinking, *My parents indulged[41] me too much. That's why I did not care to get a proper education. If I could get my childhood back, I'd waste no time and study properly.*

The Lady of Wishes happened to be passing that way. She came to know their wishes and said to herself, *Let me grant their wishes for a while and see what happens.*

She appeared before the father and told him that he would be his son's age and to the son she granted his wish to be his father's age.

Early in the morning old Subalchandra jumped out of bed. He found that he had become short, got back all his teeth and there was no sign of any beard and moustache. The clothes he had worn the night before were much too big for him. As a result, the free end of his dhoti trailed on the ground making it difficult for him to even walk.

Our Sushilchandra who used to get up to his pranks as soon as he was out of bed, could not get up this morning. At least his father's hue and cry[42] made him, wake up. His clothes had become so tight that they were bursting at the seams. He had a grey beard and moustache covering half his face and his thick

---

41 Pampered
42 Outcry

hair was replaced by a shining bald pate[43].

Both of them had been granted their wishes, but the transformation caused a lot of trouble. Sushil had wanted to be like his father for the freedom it would give him to do what he liked. He had thought of climbing trees, diving into pools, eating green mangoes and roaming around. But surprisingly that morning he wanted to do none of these things. Instead, he rolled out a mat on the porch and sat down thinking to himself.

Then it occurred to him that he should not give up all games and tried to climb a tree nearby. The day before he had climbed this tree like a squirrel, but he could not do it today! He tried to get hold of a young branch which gave way and old Sushil fell on the ground with a thud. Passersby started laughing seeing the old man get up to childish pranks. Sushilchandra felt mortified, sat down on the mat and called out to the servant, "Go and fetch me a rupee's worth of toffees."

Sushil had always been very fond of toffees. Whenever he had a little money he bought sweets from the shop near the school.

He had dreamt of stuffing his pockets with sweets when he had a lot of money like his father. The servant brought him a full one rupee's worth of sweets. He put one in his toothless mouth and started sucking it. But the old man did not care for children's sweets any more. He thought, *Let me give these to my child-father.*

But he decided against it thinking, *Eating so many sweets might make him sick.*

All the boys who had played games with him even the day before, ran away when they saw old Sushil.

_____

43 A person's head

Sushil had thought if he were independent like his father, he would play games with his friends the whole day. But today the sight of his friends irritated him. *I'm sitting here in peace and these boys have come to bother me, he thought.*

Earlier, Subal had sat on the mat and brooded over the time he had wasted as a child and thought of making up for the lost time if he got his boyhood back.

But now that Subal's wish had been granted, the very thought of going to school was distasteful to him. When an irritated Sushil would come and say, "Aren't you going to school, Dad?"

Subal would scratch his head and mumble, "I've got a tummy ache."

This annoyed Sushil and he would say, "I know all those ploys[44] for not going to school. I had them too."

Of course, Sushil knew so many tricks, that his father could not give him the slip so easily. Sushil forced his little father to go to school. As soon as Subal returned from school old Sushil would read the Ramayan aloud and make Subal sit in front, and do the sums. In the evening other old men joined Sushil to play a game of chess. Sushil engaged a private tutor to give Subal lessons during that time, and the coaching continued until late at night.

Sushil also remembered that when his father had been old, he had indigestion whenever he overate. So he did not allow him to eat a big meal. But Subal was young now and had an enormous appetite. He could have digested stones. With the frugal[45] meals he was allowed, he grew thin and his bones started to stick out. Now this made Sushil think that there was something seriously wrong with him and he stuffed him with

44 Tactics
45 Economical

all kinds of medicines and tonics.

Old Sushil also faced a number of problems. All the things he loved doing as a boy no longer agreed with him. Earlier he never missed an opportunity to go to a theatrical show. When he tried doing the same now, he would come down with a bad cold and aches and pains which kept him in bed for several weeks. He had always taken a dip in the pond. But when he did so now, his rheumatism became so acute that it took him six months to recover. After this he bathed once every two days in warm water and did not allow Subal to take a dip in the pond. Now for Sushil jumping out of bed meant aches and pains in the bones. If he took a paan, he soon realised he had no teeth to chew it with. If ever his old habit made him hurl a stone at Aunt Andi's earthen pot, people came to chide[46] the old man for such childish pranks. He did not know how to hide his utter embarrassment.

Sometimes Subalchandra forgot how young he looked. Thinking himself as old as before, he would turn up where old men sat playing cards or dice and started talking like a grown-up. They would pull his ears and send him away saying, "Enough of your impertinence[47]. Now, go and play."

At other times he would say to his teacher, "Give me the hookah, I'd like a smoke." The teacher would think him insufferably cheeky and tell him to stand on one leg as punishment for his misbehaviour.

If he complained to the barber that the latter had not come to give him a shave for days, the barber would retort saying, "I'll come in ten years' time."

Out of old habit sometimes Subal tried to discipline Sushil

---

46 Criticise or blame

by hitting him. Sushil would lose his temper and shout, "How dare you hit an old man? Is this what you learn at school?" And people would come and scold and thrash him for insolence[47].

At last, Subal started praying hard, *I wish I were old like my son Sushil and free to do what I liked.*

Likewise Sushil would pray, *Oh God, make me young like my father so that I can play to my heart's content. I can no longer control my father. I keep worrying about the next mischief hell get up to.*

The Lady of Wishes appeared before them once again and asked, "Have you had enough of your wishes?"

They both greeted her with bowed heads and said, "We've had enough, mother. Now let's be what we were before."

The Lady of Wishes said, "All right. From tomorrow morning, you two will be as you were before."

Next morning Subal woke up the old man, and Sushil found himself the boy he used to be. They both felt as if they had been dreaming.

Subal said gravely, "Aren't you going to work on your grammar lesson?"

Sushil scratched his head and said, "Dad, I've lost my book."

---

47 Cheekiness

The Runaway

Motilal Babu, zamindar of Kanthalia, was returning home with his family by boat. At midday they moored[48] near a market town for lunch when a young Brahmin boy, not more than 15-16, came up, and asked Moti Babu, "Where are you going?"

"To Kanthalia," replied Moti Babu.

The boy asked if he could be dropped at Nandigram. Motilal Babu agreed and asked his name.

"Tarapada," the boy replied.

Tarapada was a good-looking boy. He wore a shabby dhoti, and did not cover the upper part of his body which was lean and firm. He had large eyes, smiling lips and a delicate youthful charm.

Motilal Babu took an instant liking to the boy, and invited him to have lunch with his family after he had his bath.

Tarapada said, "Wait". He promptly set about helping the cook and finished cooking in no time. Then he bathed in the river, put on a clean dhoti, combed his long hair, and presented himself to Motilal Babu.

Motilal Babu went inside the boat and introduced the boy to his wife Annapurna and their nine-year-old daughter Charushashi. Annapurna's heart went out to this handsome boy and she wondered where he had come from, and how his mother could bear parting from him. At lunch the boy ate frugally[49] despite Annapurna's affectionate attention and insistence that he eat a little more. He did exactly as he wished, but with such grace that it did not seem wilful[50] or offensive[51].

Tarapada was an unusual boy. He was the fourth son of his parents. His father had died when he was very young. He was everyone's favourite. All showered affection on him. Although he had no reason to leave home, one day he ran off with a troupe of travelling performers. After a long search, when he was found and brought back, he was showered with affection and gifts instead of being scolded.

Tarapada was not to be tied down, not even by the bonds of love. He would watch the changing scenes – boats being towed along the river, a holy man resting under a huge banyan tree or a group of gypsies going about their chores. All these made him long for the great and unknown world beyond the confines of his village. After he had run away a few more times, his family and neighbours finally gave up on him.

First he had joined a troupe of players. All the members of the troupe, even the people of the houses where they performed, doted on him. But one day he disappeared without a trace.

Tarapada had music in his blood. He was drawn to the troupe of players because of their songs which set his veins throbbing.

The leader took great care in teaching him to sing. He learnt a few songs and then was gone.

Tarapada's last stop had been a band of gymnasts. He had

---

49 Economically
50 Deliberate, done intentionally
51 Unpleasant

taught himself to play the flute and played light classical tunes of thumris as the gymnasts performed at various fairs during the months of June and July. This was the group he had left when he heard that the zamindars of Nandigram were setting up a folk theatre group. He was on his way to Nandigram when he met Motilal Babu.

After lunch, the boat set sail again and Tarapada climbed up to the roof of the cabin to escape further questioning by Annapurna about his home and family. From here he could watch the ever-changing panorama of nature and give a helping hand to the boatmen when they had a break.

They passed two-three days on the river. Tarapada was always on hand to help out with cooking, shopping and even rowing.

One evening Motilal Babu was reading the episode of Kush and Luv from the Ramayana to his wife and daughter. Tarapada came down from the roof and said, "Let me sing this one for you."

He started singing the story of Kush and Luv. His voice was clear and melodious and the boatmen and travellers on nearby boats listened to him intently. When he ended, his audience was sad that it was over so soon.

Annapurna's heart grew fonder, and Motilal Babu wished he could keep the boy with him for good to make up for the lack of a son. All this made Charushashi jealous, and she hated the boy.

Charushashi was the only child of her parents. She was wilful and full of whims[52], and her mother's indulgence made her worse. Her jealousy and hatred for Tarapada made her

---

52 Sudden and unusual desire or idea

more unhappy, and she found fault with almost everything her parents did to please her. Realising that her daughter was jealous, Annapurna stopped showing her affection for the boy in her presence.

Charushashi's dark flashing eyes, her quick temper amused Tarapada and he tried to win her over by telling her stories, singing songs, playing the flute and everything he could think of. But nothing worked. It was only in the afternoon that she watched him with curiosity and interest as he swam effortlessly in the river with his fair and strong body moving in the waves like a water god. But she pretended to be indifferent and continued knitting a scarf.

At one point they passed Nandigram, but Tarapada showed no interest. Finally, after ten days, the big boat reached Kanthalia and the zamindar and his family were given a noisy welcome complete with gunshot fired into the air. While all this was going on, Tarapada stepped off the boat, and took a quick survey of the village. Within a very short time he had made friends, and become an indispensable[53] part of the village by his ability to adapt to any situation.

Though Tarapada had won the whole village over, Charushashi with her jealousy and scorn[54] remained his greatest stumbling block, but unknown to Charu, some subtle changes were taking place in her heart.

A few days later Cham's best friend Sonamoni came to see her after her return. Charu had thought of impressing Sonamoni with her stories about Tarapada—their prized

---

53 Absolutely essential
54 Contempt

possession. As she started relating her story in great detail, she was dismayed to discover that Sonamoni already knew Tarapada and called him Dada. He had played the flute for her and her mother, and even made a bamboo flute at Sonamoni's request, and fetched her fruits and flowers.

Charu felt as though her heart would burst—Tarapada was their private property. Others could admire him from a distance. But why should he be so accessible[55] to people like Sonamoni?

That day Charu broke up her friendship with Sonamoni picking a row. Then she stormed into Tarapada's room, took out his flute, and smashed it to pieces stamping on it.

Tarapada entered the room in the middle of this. When asked why she was doing this, Charu reacted with flashing eyes and flushed face and said, "I want to." Then she kicked at the broken pieces, and was gone.

Tarapada picked up the useless broken pieces, and laughed. Charu was becoming more and more of an enigma[56] to him.

Tarapada was well acquainted with the world around him, but the picture books in Motilal Babu's library fascinated him by their strangeness. Motilal Babu noticed his fascination, and asked, "Would you like to learn English? Then you'll know what these picture books mean."

Tarapada said, "Yes."

Motilal Babu engaged the headmaster of the village high school to give English lessons to Tarapada every evening. Tarapada was now completely engrossed in his new-found interest, and was hardly seen wandering round the village.

Charu suddenly expressed her desire to learn English. Her

55 Reachable
56 Puzzle

parents tried to laugh it off, but had to give in[57] when she became tearful.

Charu was too restless to learn from any book. She learnt nothing, but disturbed Tarapada's studies. She would creep in, steal Tara's pens, tear his book or pour ink over his notebooks—Tarapada bore most of this in good humour. Sometimes he found it unbearable, but she could not be controlled.

At last Tarapada hit upon a way out. One day he found his notebook so spoilt that he tore it up, and sat looking glum. When Cham came, he ignored her completely, but continued to sit silently. This was something new for Charu. She was penitent[58], and wanted to apologise, but did not know how to.

Finally, she wrote on a piece of paper in large letters, "I'll never pour ink on your book again." When Tarapada saw this, he burst out laughing.

Charu was overcome with shame and anger, and ran out of the room, wishing she could undo what she had done.

Charu and her friend Sonamoni agreed over most things, but when it came to Tarapada, Charu was not prepared to compromise. She particularly objected to his occasional visits to Sonamoni's mother. She threatened Tarapada that she would tell her father that he was neglecting his studies. When her threats did not work, one evening she even locked up Tarapada in his room, and opened the door only at dinner time. When Charu found him angry and he refused to eat, she begged him to forgive her and promised never to do the same again. When nothing worked, she started weeping. Tarapada relented, and agreed to eat.

---

57 Yield to
58 Repentant

Although Charu promised many times over to behave herself and not to tease or trouble Tarapada, when Sonamoni or anything else came between her and Tarapada, she lost her self-control. The same pattern of angry outbursts, followed by tears and then a short interlude of peace became the norm.

Nearly two years passed and it seemed as if Tarapada was at last beginning to settle down.

Charu was by this time 11 and of marriageable age. Motilal Babu started looking for a suitable match for his daughter. Once he even arranged for some people from a good family to come and see Charu. But Charu threw a fit, and refused to appear before her prospective in-laws.

Motilal Babu realized that it might not be easy to get his wilful and rebellious daughter married. Annapurna came to his rescue and suggested Tarapada as a suitable groom for Charu. The idea appealed to him as it meant that he would not have to send off his daughter to someone else's house.

A messenger was sent to Tarapada's village. He returned with the news that Tarapada's lineage was good but the family was poor. A formal proposal of marriage was sent to Tarapada's mother and elder brother. They were overjoyed and lost no time in sending their consent.

Motilal Babu and Annapurna started their preparation for the wedding in earnest. A date was fixed in Shravana. Motilal Babu instructed his lawyer in Kolkata to hire an English band and sent him a shopping list.

Charu still continued with her antics. Motilal Babu arranged for Tarapada's family to be brought over from their village, but said nothing to him.

Clouds started gathering for another monsoon and suddenly the rains came. A new wave of life and hope swept through the villages on either side of the river renewing nature as well as trade. Children danced and played on the riverbank and women came out as if to greet an old friend.

This was the time for a famous fair. On a moonlit night Tarapada came to the riverbank and watched the boats, carrying a troupe of actors, different kinds of merchandise, bands playing music, boatmen rending the sky with their noisy drums and cymbals. Gradually dark clouds moved in from the eastern sky and covered the moon. The thunder began to rumble, lightning flashed across the sky and from the depth of darkness came the scent of torrential rain. Only the village of Kanthalia lay sleeping.

The next day Tarapada's mother and brother arrived in Kanthalia. Three large boats loaded with various goods moored near the treasury of the zamindar.

Sonamoni came early in the morning and waited timidly with a little pickle and mango jelly in front of Tarapada's study. But Tarapada was nowhere to be seen. Before the ties of love and affection could encircle him completely he was lost again on a rainy night and gone to the aloof world at large.

Shiburam

The sun had just set on the horizon as I could see across the field stretching several miles before me. It had also gone dark overhead and soon the darkness began moving west and descending slowly on the western end of the field. At this dusk[59] the full moon appeared on the east and its feeble light spread over the field and created an atmosphere between light and shade. I sat in the middle of the field, but not far from my farmer's bungalow and watched the daylight fade from mid-heaven down on the western horizon and, finally, disappear into the darkness beyond. A gentle summer evening breeze was blowing when a fox appeared suddenly before me in the field.

"Old brother," uttered the fox and surprised me with his human tongue. "You have made yourself too busy in your fatherly duty. Although you are engaged most of the day with your work in the field, you give quite a lot of time to your children's upbringing. May I know why I am neglected like this?" asked the fox.

The sudden appearance of a fox before me in the eerie[60] atmosphere of light and shade in the field had already surprised me enough and the human words from the mouth of a beast astonished me further.

59 The time of the day after sunset but before night
60 Mysterious

"What do you wish me to do?" I asked, after a little pause.

"It's true I am a beast," said the fox, "but can't you help me shed my animality? I am determined to be brought up by you."

By now the light of the full moon had fallen on the fox's face which was not clearly visible. I kept gazing at the face and pondering over his words and thought to myself, This beast has given me nice service indeed.

"How did you come upon this brilliant idea?" I asked. "Why do you think you need human education?"

"If I become human with proper human education," said the fox, "I'll be famous in the entire population of the foxes. And all the foxes will worship me as a great human."

"Very good!" said I.

I informed all my friends about the fox who had appeared before me at dusk in the field under the light of the full moon and what he had said to me. My friends seemed very happy.

"Indeed it is a work that has great rewards," said my friends. "It will do a lot of good to the world."

My friends and I called a meeting and between us we founded a club and named it the 'Fox Reformation Society.' We were all farmers engaged in various agricultural occupations and we lived on the land where all relevant agricultural work was undertaken by us. It was difficult to find a suitable building for the address of the club as most buildings were bungalows occupied by the farming families in various parts of the field. At last we thought of the place situated in the middle of the agricultural tract and generally known as the market or assembly and regularly used for assessing our everyday farm produce. As the assembly finished its work around seven o'clock every evening, we arranged for a regular sitting for the club around

nine o'clock. We supped between 7.30-8.30 and sauntered[61] into the assembly house a little before nine o'clock, the time appointed for the fox to appear before the club every evening.

The fox had just entered and sat on his haunches[62] on the floor immediately before us, sitting in a row. The light of the moon fell on his entire body and the stars in both his eyes twinkled although his head, face and the rest of the body remained largely misty.

"Son, what do your relatives call you?" asked I.

"Haw-haw," answered the fox and it seemed he raised his head higher because he was very proud of his name which was appropriate for a leader and too flattering for an ordinary mortal which Haw-haw was certain he was.

"No! No!" said we clearly in chorus. "It won't do. If you wish to be an educated human, you must first change your name. And also you'll have to alter your appearance so that there can be no difference between you and the others, that is, the human and the educated. So from now you are Shiburam as it's the name we have bestowed upon you just now, and remember always that you have no other name but only Shiburam."

Of course, Shiburam had never been taught the usual traditions which began at birth as a part of human upbringing with such practices as baptism, naming for the new born, various forms of initiation and the first few stages in induction. Indeed he had not expected that his education would begin with a naming ceremony. The new name had, however, not at all pleased him which we guessed when he opened his mouth full, exposing all his teeth glistening in the moonlight, immediately

---

61 Strolled
62 The thighs and buttocks of people and animals

upon the naming. We conjectured[63] that he must have thought that Haw-haw was always the happiest name he could ever have had as one of the most respectable members of his community.

"All right," said Shiburam almost rudely and closed his mouth. It seemed that he thought he had no choice and he must be educated and become human.

Our first job was to make Shiburam stand on his hind legs. He took a long time to learn. He began like a toddler and needed quite a lot of support from us to keep him steady on his two legs at the back but now and again he kept falling over. Eventually, it took him six months to learn to stand like adult humans keeping himself erect. At this time we thought of covering his paws, putting on a pair of gloves on his front paws and socks and shoes on his hind paws. All members of the club felt reasonably satisfied with what our training had so far achieved.

"Shiburam, now take a look at the image of your two-footed carriage in the mirror and say if you like it," Gaur Goswami, the president of the club, said at last.

Shiburam stood in front of the mirror, looked at himself from different angles, turned right and tried to assess what his left looked like, turned and bent his head and neck before and sideways to judge what his back looked like and gave a lot of time to such considerations.

"Goswamiji, even now I can't see any resemblance between your features and mine," said Shiburam very slowly but also very thoughtfully.

"Is that all, Shibu?" said Goswamiji. "Is it enough to be upright only? It's not easy to become human, you know. I say, what do you do with your tail? Can you give up your great love for the tail?"

---

63 Guessed

Shiburam's face fell as the skin had suddenly become too dry because the blood which had kept its fresh look had quietly evaporated from the textures. He could not help remembering that in more than 20 villages in the fox country his was the most famous tail of all tails. He took two whole days to consider the proposal and could not sleep at all for three nights.

At last, he called at the club at nine o'clock in the evening on Thursday and said, "Yes, I want to get rid of the tail." And the ginger coloured tail with fluffy hair was at once cut off very close from the stem.

"Aha, what a freedom for an animal," said all members in unison. "At last he has been freed from the bondage of a tail. What a blessing! What fulfilment!"

Shiburam took a deep breath very quietly and fell into a pensive[64] mood. His eyes were filled with tears, but somehow he managed to hold them back and said in a very pathetic intonation[65], "What blessings."

That day he felt no desire for food and dreamed of the severed tail throughout the night. Next evening Shiburam did not fail to come to the meeting.

"Shibu, how do you do?" said Goswamiji. "Are you indeed feeling light in your body?"

"Please sir, indeed very light," said Shiburam. "But I can't help thinking that the tail is certainly gone although the difference of class with the humans has not ended."

"If you want to belong," said Goswami, "to the same class with a matching colour, remove the fluff of hair from your body."

Tinu, the barber was called and it took him five whole days to

---

64 Deeply or sadly thoughtful
65 The rise and fall of voice while speaking

scrape off the fluff of hair with a razor running it close to the skin slowly and minutely. All members fell into a deep silence in great amazement at the colour which bloomed up on the skin.

"Honourables," said a very agitated Shiburam, "Why aren't you talking at all?"

"We are astounded at our own great deed," said the members.

Shiburam, however, felt very peaceful as the slanted beam of moonlight reached into the darkness under the thatch on wooden beams settled on four wooden posts, with no walls and fell on a slant on Shiburam's entire body keeping the members before him in the dark. This gave an almost black or very grey look to their features. Looking at the humans, who would have seemed to any other human, to be ghosts sitting on wooden chairs in a row before a long but narrow wooden table, Shiburam got out of his sad feelings at the loss of the severed tail and scraped-off fluff of hair.

"That's all Shiburam, no more," said the members with their eyes closed. "The meeting is now closed."

"From now," said Shibu, "my only work is to keep the fox population continuously in a state of astonishment."

The other side of the fence showed Shiburam's aunt, his father's sister called Khekini, wandering in tears all over the country, and in the end Huk-kui, the spokesman for the village, went to their chief.

"Chief, sir," said Huk-kui, "it's more than a year and we haven't seen Haw-haw. Do you know why he is missing? Surely he has not fallen into the hands of the tigers and bears?"

"Why do you fear tigers and bears?" said the chief. "The only beast, we need fear is the humankind. Perhaps he has fallen into their traps."

The responsibility for the search for Haw-haw fell on every

fox and a body of volunteers began exploring Haw-haw's whereabouts until they arrived at the clubhouse with a thatch roof on four wooden posts without walls, in the middle of the bamboo forest.

"Huk-ka hua," called in chorus the pack of volunteer foxes of the search party.

Unaware, Shiburam had been sitting in a cluster of bamboos close to the club-house and dozing on and off. He heard the call and became wary, but his heart began pounding in excitement and he wished very much to return the call full throatedly but with great difficulty somehow managed to suppress his desire. After another two hours in the bamboo forest rose again the same call "huk-ka hua" and this time came up a suppressed little low sound of a sob in the throat. When two more hours had passed, the pack called out again and this time Shiburam could not suppress his response but howled out, "Huk-ka hua, huk-ka hua."

"I just heard Haw-haw's call," said Huk-kui. "Call out at once."

"Haw-haw," called the entire pack of foxes simultaneously.

"Shiburam," said the president as he got out of his bed at the house attached to the club building and appeared at the meeting place under the thatch roof on wooden posts.

"Haw-haw," came the call again from a little distance.

"Shiburam," warned Goswamiji again.

When the pack called for the third time, Shiburam ran out. But the foxes fled and the heroic big foxes such as Huk-kui, Ho-yo, Hu-hu and the like entered their independent holes as Shiburam had astounded the entire community of foxes with his altered appearance.

Six months passed and the most recent report said that Shiburam roamed the country over every night howling, "Where's my tail, where's my tail?" He sat on the stretcher before Goswami's bedroom with his mouth raised up and said on the hour sobbing, "Return my tail, return my tail." Goswami did not have the courage to open the door as he was too frightened in case the mad fox bit him.

Shiburam was prevented from going to the bushes with thorns, where his home was, as his relatives either fled away or came snarling to bite him. He still lived at the club-house where other than a pair of owls no birds or animals were ever sighted and even the bullies, the boys with big stature, such as Khendu, Gobar, Benchi, Dhenri and others did not venture to get the berries from the bushes[1] in their fear of ghosts.

In his language the fox wrote a rhyme with the following beginning:

> *Oh my tail, oh my tail,*
> *My foxhood for a tail!*
> *My heart will burst*
> *Now that I am an outcaste.*
> *Before my eyes I see nothing but a hazy veil,*
> *Oh my tail, oh my tail!*

"What injustice, great injustice," piped in Poopee. "But Grandpa, won't even his aunt take him into her home?"

"Don't worry about it," said I. "When his own fluff of hair has grown again, they will be able to recognise him."

"But his tail?"

"Perhaps something for growing tails will be available at the doctor's. I'll find out."

The Scientist

"I can't understand why you like Nilmoni Babu so much, Grandpa?" said Kusmi. "Women don't like men who're untidy, slovenly[66] and disorganised like him."

"That only goes to show that he is a 'real' man," Grandpa answered.

Kusmi was not convinced at all and requested uncle Bidhu to tell Grandpa of the turmoil[67] at Nilu Babu's house the day before.

Uncle Bidhu obliged and recreated the scene! News spread that Nilu Babu had lost his favourite pen. They searched everywhere, even the top of the mosquito net. At last Madhu was summoned and Nilu Babu asked him where his pen was. He had no clue. One by one it was the turn of the washerman and the barber. When the whole household had given up hope, his nephew walked in and pointed out that the pen was tucked behind one of Nilu's ears.

He snapped at his nephew and said, "You silly boy, the pen that's lost is the one I'm looking for."

When the commotion brought his wife out of the kitchen, Nilu said, "I can't find the pen I'm looking for."

---

66 Dirty, and careless
67 Disturbance

She told him to make do with the one he had got. He thought he might find one like it in Kundu's shop and offered to send Bhuto, his servant, to the shop to buy one, but now the wallet couldn't be found. This time he searched his pocket, but the wallet wasn't there. Again, first it was the washerman who denied having washed his shirt...

Osman, the tailor retorted by saying that his money must be in his iron chest.

Once more his wife intervened and pointed out that he had used the money to pay off the rent arrears.

"Is that so?" said Nilu. "But didn't the landlord serve a notice on me to vacate the premises?"

"It's after he had served the notice that you cleared the debt."

Nilu Babu was scandalised[68] and informed his wife that he had already rented Nimchand Haldar's house in Badurbagan for one-and-a half years.

Now his wife was angry and pointed out to him that he'd have to pay two rents every month.

That didn't bother him, "I can't remember whether I wrote down the full address in my notebook or not."

When his wife suggested that he look up the notebook, he said it had been missing for three days. The nephew reminded him that he had given it to his sister who had gone to stay with her uncle in Allahabad.

While Nilu was thinking how to sort out the mess, who should turn up but Nimchand Haldar's clerk! He said he had come to collect the rent on the house at Badurbagan. When asked which house that was, he said it was 13 Shibu Samaddar Lane.

Nilu Babu called out to his wife "Did you hear that? What

68 Caused public outrage

a relief! Now I know the address."

"What good will that do?" demanded his wife.

"At least I've got the address."

"So you've. But what will you do about the two rents?"

"Oh, we'll think about that later. Now I must write down the address in the notebook." He looked for the notebook.

"Oh, bother, the notebook's in Allahabad. Never mind. I'll get it by heart—13 Shibu Samaddar Lane."

This 'pen episode' was nothing compared with the uproar caused the day Nilu Babu lost one of his sandals. His wife threatened to leave for her parents' house and the servants declared that they would resign if they were accused of stealing half a pair of sandals—repaired in three places at that.

"Actually, I got to hear about it too and went over to Nilu's house to see for myself," said Grandpa.

When Grandpa heard that the sandal was not lost, but stolen, he was intrigued[69] and said, "I wonder what kind of thieves these are who go around stealing single sandals only."

"That's the point," said Nilu. "It goes to show that the price of leather has skyrocketed."

Grandpa realised that there was not much point in arguing with the man...so he agreed with him and said that he also had noticed cobblers eyeing shoes of people passing by. Grandpa did manage to pacify him that day.

Kusmi said, "How can someone be so silly?"

"Don't say such things about him," said Grandpa. "He is a brilliant mathematician."

Kusmi turned up her nose and asked, "What does he do with his maths?"

Grandpa said, "Invention! He may not be good at figuring

69 Very surprised or fascinated

out mundane[70] things like how sandals are lost, but he can easily work out many complicated calculations about the stars and planets."

Kusmi lost her patience and said, "Now I know why he's always losing things and why you're so fond of him. You like eccentric[71] people and these are the people who flock around you."

"Well! Let me tell you a secret," said Grandpa. "You think his wife is fed up with a hopeless husband like Nilu. It's exactly the opposite. She is utterly taken with his careless and slovenly ways and so am I."

70 Ordinary, normal
71 Odd, unusual

The Invention of Shoes

King Hobu lived in his palace as the king of his kingdom. His subjects were happy for what their king had given them and they thought that there was no kingdom where the subjects had comparable prosperity. Hobu was well aware that his kingdom was contented and none suffered from the want of anything. One night, however, Hobu was unable to sleep and after a long while he began wondering about the cause of his sleepless night. Suddenly, it dawned upon him that he had been wondering about a possible relation between his feet and the ground they generally trod on whenever it was necessary to walk a few steps and, finally, he decided to talk about it in the morning with Gobu Rai, his minister.

Gobu had got up quite early and also taken his breakfast. After breakfast he looked at the clock on the wall before his breakfast table to see if it was the right time to visit the king. Gobu went to the king's sitting room and found him on a sofa with his feet tucked under the legs.

As soon as the king saw Gobu before him, he said, "Listen Gobu Rai. All day yesterday and throughout the night I thought why my feet should get dusty as soon as I step on the ground?"

By the time Hobu had spoken his first words, Gobu's assistants too had appeared on the scene and stood quite close to him. Hobu's words made Gobu and others wonder what the

king really meant and all gave out various sounds individually and collectively. Meanwhile Hobu continued, "You lot only take your wages and never attend to the king's duty at all. What irregularity is this in my own kingdom that my own land smears me with dust! Find a remedy at once or I will punish you all!"

When Gobu heard the king, he started to think hard. His worries made him nervous and he got so scared that his whole body broke out in cold sweat. The king's question seemed to have disturbed many others at the palace. The learned scholars lost the usual glow of wisdom on their faces and the most obedient servants were unable to sleep at night. In the kitchen none put the pan on the fire as the palace was filled with weeping and tears rolled down the cook's cheeks and tears also ran from Gobu's eyes down his white beard...Gobu put his head on the ground immediately before Hobu's feet and said, "If your feet do not take the dust, how do we get the dust from your own feet!"

The king heard, closed his mouth and eyes and became ponderous as something passed through his head. Gobu and his men did not understand what was going on, why Hobu had closed his eyes or whether he had fallen asleep.

Suddenly, Hobu began rocking his body. He opened his eyes and said, "That's true, but get rid of the dust. Think of the philosophy later. Are the feet and the dust the same?"

Gobu said, "But we must take the dust. Do we take the feet instead, or what?"

Gobu's assistants said, "Yes, yes, very true, dust or feet, feet or dust..."

Hobu said, "On the other hand, if you don't get the dust from my feet because there are only the feet and no dust, you will take your wages for nothing."

Gobu said, "But we don't take our wages for nothing."

Hobu said, "Listen Gobu and you all, why do I keep so many servants and scientists with the highest degrees? Fulfil first your first duty and think of the 'after' much later."

The king's words made the minister see darkness before him and with great care he collected all highly qualified and wise scientists, engineers, technicians and craftsmen in the land and overseas and brought them to the king's notice. All put on their glasses, took their seats, sniffed up 19 barrels of snuff, blew up heavy clouds of snuff into the air and, after much hard thinking, said, "Where will the crops grow without the soil?"

The king said, "If that's impossible, what are these scientists for?"

The scientists looked vacantly before them for a while, nodded their heads a few times, reasoned between them very thoughtfully and in the end ordered the purchase of 17 lakh and 50 thousand brooms, and from the brooms' hard sweep the dust on the road blew up and covered entirely the king's features and the chest. None could open their eyes in the dust, the sun was covered with a cloud of dust, before the blowing force of the dust the people coughed their life out and the entire city disappeared into the clouds of dust and ceased to exist.

The king said, "You tried to get rid of the dust. Instead you have filled the world entirely with dust!"

Immediately, 21 lakh water-porters with leather skin water carriers on their arms were ordered to run speedily in swarms and the ponds and water holes were left only with mud and no boat could move even on the water of the rivers. Life in the water died from the loss of water and the creatures on the land tried to learn swimming. The merchandise sank into the bottom of the mud, the entire land began suffering from cold and fever.

The king said, "Such stupid idiots, they have killed the dust to turn it into watery mud."

Again all called for a conference, every qualified person took his seat; their heads seemed to spin round and they saw nothing before them and never found an end to the dust.

The scientists were sitting amidst a crowd of royal officers and lazy observers who had been perplexed with the results from the scientific advice and by now a commotion arose in the crowd. Quickly some scientists said, "Cover the earth with matting and we will hold back dust under an overlap."

Some others said, "Keep the king at home. See there's no opening through which dust can enter. If he does not put his feet in the middle of the dust, they will not touch his feet."

The people around the scientists liked the advice so much that they produced at once quite an uproar[72] of approval with all sorts of sounds which were largely unintelligible but taken certainly for universal agreement. The king remained silent for a very long time and refrained from making any comment immediately, because he argued silently to himself on the advantages and disadvantages which were hidden in the advice and whether the advice would help his subjects more and him less and what sort of result would follow from it.

In the end, the king said very slowly but quite audibly without however knowing whether he spoke to himself or his

---

72 A noisy disturbance or confusion

advisers, "That's a great truth," and paused for a few minutes. He repeated, "That's a great truth," and added, "but my mind has doubts..." and paused again for a while. At last, he said firmly and loudly, "If I am shut in day and night from the world outside because I am weary of the mud, I am afraid, my kingdom will turn into mud."

The scientists said immediately, "In that case call the leatherman and cover the earth in leather."

Some in the crowd began shouting, "A leatherman, a leatherman, my money for a leatherman. Where's the leatherman? Get the leather, get the skin, our king will reward the earth and the leatherman for giving the naked earth a nice mantle."

The others said, "Covering the earth of dust under a curtain will make the great deed of the king of the earth last for ever."

All, however, said immediately, "It can be done easily if we find a proper leatherman."

The king's men went on circulating his command to bring the proper leatherman to his notice and travelling the roads in towns and cities and even the muddy lanes in villages and, prompted by their companion, the town crier, produced such a noise everywhere with drums, pipes and cymbals that a large number of the countrymen began thinking very seriously if they should all flee the land immediately. The proper leatherman was available nowhere, nor was the appropriate quantity of skin. In the end an aged leatherman and, by his own word, the supposed chief of the leatherman clan entered the king's hall slowly, approached the king's presence with his head bowed very low, stood before him, bowed his head even lower and said with a very short and hardly audible, very dry laugh, "If permission is kindly granted, I can say what will fulfil the desire easily. Cover your own two feet and it will be no longer necessary to cover the earth."

The crowd in the hall roared in anger and howled at the old leatherman. "Are you a leatherman or what? Say at once if you can remove the dust or not. We don't want to know what you think of the king's feet or any other feet."

The king gestured for silence and said, "Peace." He muttered, "Will it be so easy!" He said clearly to the audience, "Is it so easy when all the land is already under the dead weight of thinking?"

The minister said, "Keep the trifler shut in prison with shackles."

The old man sat facing the king's feet and enveloped them neatly in a cover of leather.

Gobu Rai, the minister, said, "I also had thought so. Somehow the fellow has found it out."

From that day began the custom of wearing shoes. Gobu was forgiven and the earth was rescued.

A 'Good' Man

"What a pity! I'm too good-natured."

"What's so special about it?" Kusmi said. "Who doesn't know that you're a 'good' man? By the way, what's your definition of a 'good' man?"

"Now you've asked the right question!" said Grandpa. "A 'good' man is one who gives up what's his by right not because he is generous but because he lacks courage."

"Like what?"

Grandpa said that it had happened that very morning. Kusmi was all ears and Grandpa related the incident.

"I had just settled down to write when Panchkadi appeared on the scene. It was as if the hot winds had blown over from the Sahara withering all my fresh thoughts and feelings.

"He promptly made himself comfortable on the cot where I sit and write. The 'good' man could not say that he was going to sit and work there.

"Panchkadi started recounting our school days including the saga of Govinda, the lame sweet maker. Suddenly, I noticed that my golden fountain pen was slowly moving towards his pocket under cover of his shawl. I could have said, 'That's my pen not yours.'

"But how could I? I am a 'good' man, a gentleman's son.

How could I speak of such an embarrassing thing? I couldn't even look at his thieving hand.

"I had a strong suspicion that he would say, 'I think I'll have my lunch here today.' I could not say that it wouldn't be possible.

"Suddenly, I had a bright idea. I blurted out, 'I'll have to go to Ramen's at once.'

"Panchkadi said, 'Just as well. Let's go together. I haven't met him ever since leaving school.'

"Oh bother! I flopped down. I looked out and said, 'It is raining.'

"He said, 'No problem. I don't have an umbrella. I'll come with you and share the umbrella.' Anyone else in my position would have said that was not possible.

"But the 'good' man—I couldn't. Instead I said, 'That won't be necessary. It'd be better if you took my umbrella. Return it at your convenience.'

"He jumped at the idea and said, 'A good idea!'

"He picked up the umbrella and made a hasty exit, afraid that I might suddenly start looking for my pen. The umbrella won't return, nor the pen, but the most comforting thought is that nor will he."

"What are you saying, Grandpa? You won't get back your umbrella and your fountain pen?"

"Not going by the code of conduct of a 'good' man."

"I'm not a 'good' person. I'll write to him."

"You can't do that. Moreover, what's the use? He'll say he didn't take them."

"I know he'll say that. But I want him to know that we know that he has stolen them."

"Oh God! I don't want him to know that. A gentleman's son, a thief. What a shame! I've lost so many things this way.

"You were not even born when I lost my favourite copy of Browning's poems. A book-lover friend borrowed it against my wish. When he didn't return it, I asked my local book seller to get me another copy. After some time he got me a copy. I found that it was my own book with the title page which had my name written on it, torn out. I paid and bought the book. After that I had to hide the book as if I was the thief in case he found it while browsing in my library. I didn't want him to know that I had discovered his hidden talent. After all, he's a gentleman."

"That's enough Grandpa. Now I am very clear on who is a 'good' man!..."

Return of the Little Master

Raicharan was 12 when he entered the family to work as a servant in his master's house. He was asked to look after his master's little son, Anukul. With the years, the boy started going to school. From school he went on to college for his graduation, and then he joined the judicial[73] service. Until the time he got married, Raicharan was his sole attendant.

But when a young mistress entered the house, Raicharan knew that now he had two masters, not one. The new mistress held a pivotal[74] position. Before long, there was a new arrival in the family. Anukul had a son, and Raicharan by his caring attentions soon had complete hold over the child.

And then the baby boy started crawling and would want to venture[75] outside the house. When Raicharan went after him, he would scream with naughty laughter and try to sneak away. Raicharan was amazed at the intelligence and fine judgement the baby showed when chased. He would say to his mistress admiringly, "Your son will be a judge some day."

Each day brought a pleasant surprise for all those around the child. It was nothing short of an epoch[76] making event in human history to Raicharan when the baby turned a toddler.

---

73 Related to the administration of justice
74 Crucial
75 Go (in the context of this story)
76 A particular period of time

When he called his father 'Ba-ba' and his mother 'Ma-ma' and Raicharan 'Chan-na', Raicharan was at the top of the world.

After a while Raicharan had to show his ingenuity[77] in other ways. He had, for example, to be a horse, holding the reins between his teeth, and prancing on his feet. He also had to wrestle with his little master: and if he could not, by a wrestler's trick, fall on his back defeated at the end, the battle just wouldn't stop!

Around this time, Anukul was transferred to a district on the banks of the river Padma. On his way through Kolkata he bought his son a little go-cart, a yellow satin waist-coat, a gold-laced cap, and gold bracelets and anklets. Raicharan loved taking out the finery for his little master whenever they went out, and he did it ceremoniously[78] with great pride.

Then came the rainy season, and it rained heavily for days on end. The hungry river, like a ferocious serpent, swallowed terraces, villages, and corn fields, taking under its flood the tall grasses on the sandbanks. From time to time one could hear a deep thud as the river banks caved in. The unceasing roar of the current could be heard from far away. Loads of foam, flying past, proved to the eye the force and swiftness of the steam.

One afternoon the rain stopped. It was cloudy, but cool and bright enough. Raicharan's little boss did not want to stay indoors on such a fine afternoon. He climbed onto the go-cart. Raicharan, managing the shafts, dragged him slowly along till they reached the rice fields on the river banks. There was no one in the fields, and no boat on the stream. Across the water, the sun was setting beautifully. Amidst the stillness, the child suddenly pointed in front of him and cried, 'Chan-na! Flowers.'

77 Cleverness and originality
78 Extremely formally

At a distance stood a large kadamba tree covered with flowers. The child looked at it with greedy sparkling eyes. Raicharan knew immediately what he wanted. Only a few days ago he had made, of the flower-balls of this tree, a small go-cart and the boy had been so happy dragging it about by a string, for the entire day. Raicharan was not asked to put on the reins at all. And for this, he was promoted from being a horse to being a groom.

But Raicharan didn't want to go splashing knee-deep through the mud to reach the flowers. So he quickly pointed in the opposite direction, and cried: "Look, baby look! Look at that bird!" Amidst all sorts of funny noises he pushed the go-cart rapidly away from the tree.

But the child, destined to be a judge, couldn't be tricked so easily. The little master's mind was made up, and Raicharan had to give in. "Very well, baby," he said finally, "but stay put in the cart, I'll go and get you the flowers. Mind you, don't go near the water."

As he said this, he tucked his dhoti at the waist baring the knees, and turned towards the tree.

The moment Raicharan did this, his little master's thoughts wandered off to the forbidden water. The baby saw the river rushing by, splashing and gurgling as he went closer. It seemed as though the disobedient waves themselves were running away from a bigger Raicharan with the laughter of a thousand children. At the sight of their naughty sport, the child grew excited and restless, wanting to go. He got down stealthily from the go-cart and toddled across near the river. On the way, he picked up a small stick and leaned over the bank of the stream pretending to fish. The playful fairies of the river with their mysterious voices seemed to be inviting him to come to them...

Raicharan plucked a handful of flowers from the tree and carried them back in a fold of his dhoti, his face wreathed[79] in smiles. But when he reached the go-cart he found it empty. He looked around, but there was no one in sight. He looked back at the cart, again and again but no one was there.

At that first terrible moment, his blood froze within him. Before his eyes the whole universe swam round like a dark mist. From the depths of his broken heart he gave one piercing cry, "Master, Master, little Master!"

But no one answered, "Chan-na." No child laughed naughtily back: no squeals of delight welcomed his return. Only the river ran on with its splashing, gurgling sound as before, as though it knew nothing at all, and had no time to take notice of small accidents.

As the evening crept on, Raicharan's mistress became more and more anxious and finally set out to search. With lanterns in their hands at last, they reached the banks of the Padma. There they found Raicharan rushing up and down the fields, like a mad wind, howling in despair: 'Master, Master, little Master!'

When they got Raicharan home at last, he fell at the feet of his mistress. They shook him, and questioned him, and asked him repeatedly where he had left the child: but all he could say was that he knew nothing.

Though everyone held the opinion that river Padma had swallowed the child, there was still a faint hope left. For a band of gypsies had been noticed outside the village that afternoon, and some suspicions rested on them. The mother went so far in her maddening grief as to think it possible that Raicharan himself had stolen the child. She called him aside and begged:

79 To be surrounded by or covered in

"Raicharan, give back my baby. Take all the money you want, but give me back my child!"

Raicharan only banged his forehead with his fist in reply. His angry mistress ordered him out of the house.

Anukul tried to reason with his wife and get better of [80] her ridiculous suspicion—"Why on earth, tell me," he said, "would he do something like that?"

The mother finally muttered: "The baby wore gold ornaments... Who knows?"

It was impossible to talk to her after that.

Raicharan went back to his native village. He had no son; and there was no hope that a child would now be born to him. But it came about before the end of a year that his wife delivered a son and died in childbirth.

An overwhelming resentment rose in Raicharan's heart at the sight of this new baby. At the back of his mind was an angry suspicion that it had come as an intruder to take the place of the little master. He also thought that it would be unfair to be happy with a son of his own after what had happened to his master's little child. Indeed, had it not been for Raicharan's widowed sister, who mothered the new baby, it would not have lived long.

But gradually a change came over Raicharan's mind. The new baby began to crawl about, and venture outside the house, bent on mischief. It also showed a sweet cleverness in making its escape to safety. Its voice, its laughter and tears, its gestures, were all those of the little master. At times, when Raicharan listened to its crying, his heart suddenly thumped wildly against

---

80 Gain an advantage over

his ribs, and it seemed to him that his former little master was crying somewhere in the unknown land of death because he couldn't find his "Chan-na".

Phailna (the name Raicharan's sister gave to the new baby) soon began to talk. He learnt to say 'Ba-ba' and 'Ma-ma'. When Raicharan heard those familiar sounds the mystery suddenly became clear. The little master could not cast off the spell of his Chan-na ana had been reborn in his house.

The new baby was born soon after his little master's death.

His wife had unbelievably enough given birth to a son in middle age.

The new baby took toddling steps and called out 'Ba-ba' and 'Ma-ma' – all the signs were there – this was certainly the future judge.

Suddenly Raicharan remembered the terrible accusation of the mother. "Ah," he said to himself in amazement, "the mother's heart was right. She knew I had stolen her child."

Once he arrived at this conclusion, he was filled with remorse[81] for his mistake. He now gave himself over, body and soul, to the new baby and became his most devoted care-giver. He began to bring him up as if he was the son of a rich man. He bought a go-cart, a yellow satin waist-coat, and a gold-embroidered cap. He sold the ornaments of his dead wife and made gold amulets and anklets for the son. He refused to let the little one play with children in the neighbourhood and himself became his sole companion day and night. As the baby grew to boyhood he got spoilt, so the village children would call him 'Your Lordship', and tease him; and older people

81 Regret, guilt

regarded Raicharan as totally crazy about the child.

And then, it was time for the boy to go to school. Raicharan sold his small piece of land and went to Kolkata. There with great difficulty he found a job and sent Phailna to school. He worked very hard to give him the best education, the best clothes, the best food while, he himself lived on a handful of rice and muttered secretly – "Ah, my little master, my dear little master, you loved me so much that you came back to my house. You will never suffer from any neglect of mine."

Twelve years passed away. The boy could now read and write well. He was bright, good-looking, enjoying good health. He paid a great deal of attention to his looks and took extra care of his hair. He was extravagant, and spent money freely on finery and enjoyment. He never could regard Raicharan quite as a father because, though he got his affection, there was something servile[82] about his attitude towards him. Moreover, Raicharan kept it totally secret that he was the father of the child.

The other students in Phailna's hostel would be amused by Raicharan's uncouth[83] ways, and behind his father's back Phailna joined in their fun. But, at the bottom of their hearts, all the students loved the innocent and tender-hearted old man, and Phailna too was very fond of him. But, as I have said before, he loved him in a patronising[84] way.

Raicharan grew older and older and his employer was increasingly finding faults with him. He nearly starved himself

---

82 Overanxious to please
83 Lacking good manners
84 Treating somebody as inferior

for the boy's sake, growing weak in body and was no longer up to his usual chores. He began to forget things and had slowed down. But his boss expected full returns of the wages, not willing to put up with excuses. The money that Raicharan had brought with him from the sale of his land was now over and the boy continually grumbled about his clothes, asking for more.

At last Raicharan made up his mind. He quit his job, and left some money with Phailna. Before leaving, he told Phailna that he was going away on an urgent business to his native village, he would return soon after.

He went off at once to Barasat where Anukul was magistrate. Anukul's wife still lived under the ominous[85] shadow of the grief for she had no other child.

One evening Anukul was resting after a long and weary day in court. His wife was buying an exorbitant herb from a roaming quack. He had promised her that it would give her a child. Suddenly, in the courtyard, Anukul heard a voice in greeting, so he went out to see who was there. It was good old Raicharan! Anukul's heart went out to him instantly. He asked him many questions, and offered to take him back in his earlier job.

But Raicharan just smiled vaguely and said: "I only wanted to pay my regards to my mistress."

Anukul accompanied Raicharan into the house, but the mistress did not receive him as warmly as his old master had done. Raicharan ignored that and with his hand folded in appeal, said, "It was not the river Padma that stole your baby.

---

85 Threatening

It was I."

"Good God!" Anukul exclaimed. "What! Where is he?"

Raicharan replied, "He is with me. I will bring him the day after tomorrow."

It was Sunday, and from early morning both husband and wife were gazing expectantly along the road, waiting for Raicharan. At around ten, he came, leading Phailna by the hand.

Anukul's wife, without questioning his identity, took the boy on her lap and was besides herself in excitement, laughing, weeping, touching him, kissing his hair, arid his forehead, and taking in eagerly all she could with hungry, eager eyes. The boy was very good-looking and dressed like a gentleman's son. Anukul's heart welled up with a sudden gush of affection.

Nevertheless the magistrate in him asked: "Have you any proof that he is my son?"

Raicharan said: "Proof? What proof of such a deed? God alone knows that I and no one else in the world stole your boy."

When Anukul saw how eagerly his wife clung to the boy, he realized how futile[86] it was to ask for proofs. It would be wiser to believe. And then — where could an old man like Raicharan get such a fine boy? And why should his faithful servant deceive him? He could surely hope for no gain from such deceit!

Still, he could not forget his old servant's lapse in duty. He announced, "Raicharan, you must not remain here any longer."

"Where shall I go, Master?" said Raicharan, in a voice choking with grief.

Then with folded hands he added, "I am old. Who will give an old man a job?"

The mistress said, "Let him stay. My child will be pleased,

---

86 Of no use

and I forgive him." But Anukul's magisterial conscience would not permit this.

"No," he said, "he cannot be forgiven for what he has done."

Raicharan fell to the ground and clasped Anukul's feet. "Master," he cried, "allow me to stay on. It was not I who did it, it was God!"

Anukul was more shocked than ever when Raicharan tried to put the blame on God.

"No," he said, "I can't allow this. I can't trust you any more. You have been cruel and unfair."

Raicharan rose to his feet and said, "It was not I who did it."

"Who was it then?" asked Anukul.

Raicharan replied, "It was my fate."

But no educated man could buy this for an excuse, and Anukul remained firm. When Phailna came to know that he was the wealthy magistrate's son, and not Raicharan's, he was at first upset, for he thought that he had been cheated all these years of his birthright. But seeing Raicharan in distress, he generously said to Anukul, "Father, please forgive him. Even if you don't let him live with us, let him at least have a small monthly pension."

Hearing this, Raicharan was speechless. He looked for the last time at the face of his son. He bowed to his old master and mistress. Then he went out and mingled with the innumerable people of the world.

At the end of the month, Anukul sent some money to his village. But the money came back, for no person of the name Raicharan lived there anymore.

QUESTIONS

Kabuliwala

1. How do you know that Mini was a talkative and restless girl? Give two examples from the text.
2. "Now he will come in, and my 17th chapter will never get finished!"
   (a) Who said these words and when?
   (b) Who is the "he" referred to in this sentence?
3. The Kabuliwala regularly gave Mini some gifts. What were they?
4. Describe the article that the Kabuliwala carried to remind him of his daughter?
5. What was common between the author and the Kabuliwala? Write three sentences about each of them.

Give reasons

1. Mini was a patient listener.
2. The author's heart throbbed with pain.
3. The doting father had to give up on several festivities and decorations that he had planned for his daughter's wedding. Yet the wedding was brighter and he was happy.

Formative Questions

1. Find out more about 'Kabuliwalas'? What were they known for?
2. Discuss with your partner:
   Mini's mother had certain fears about the Kabuliwala. Does your mother have similar fears about you? Give a few examples.
3. Group Activity: In three minutes, enact a portion of the lesson that you liked most.

4.   Fill in the blanks using key words/phrases from the lesson:-

(a)   There was a _____ to kill the leader of the tribe.

(b)   January 30 is observed as Martyr's Day __ _____ __ Mahatma Gandhi.

(c)   The _____ waves caused great harm to the shops on the seashore.

(d)   'Pass away' is a _____ for 'die.'

(e)   The little boy's _____ was all about his new play station.

The Parrot's Training

Summative Questions

1.   Why did people believe that the bird was ignorant?

2.   What do you understand by "Culture, captured and caged!"

3.   Describe the tower of culture.

4.   How was the king welcomed at the great Hall of Learning?

5.   "The scribes with light hearts and heavy pockets hurried home". Why were their hearts light and their pockets heavy?

6.   Write the essence of the story in two lines.

Formative Questions

1.   Write the essence of the story in 2 lines.

2.   Find out the meaning of the phrase 'bird brain'. Who do you think had a bird brain in this story?

3.   If you were a parrot, would you prefer to be well fed but caged, or be free? Why?

The Rat's Feast

Summative Questions
1. Where were the boys returning from?
2. An elderly gentleman got into the train. What was he carrying?
3. Complete the sentences
   (a) The old man got off at Asansol to ....
   (b) All the sweets in the pots had been...................
   (c) The boy thought that it would have been great fun it they could see the ....
4. Why do you think the story is called "The Rat's Feast"?
5. What kind of a teacher do you think Mr. Tarkalankar would have been? Complete your answer within three sentences.

Formative Questions
1. Be honest with this one! Do you give nicknames to your teachers? Write two names that you have given your teachers. You need not mention their actual names .

Atonement

Summative Questions
Match the words with their meanings
(a)	Atonement	indifferently
(b)	Industrious	money paid as salary to a trainee
(c)	Nonchalantly	correct/rectify
(d)	With flying colours	compensation for a sin or a crime
(e)	Make amends	very successfully
(f)	Stipend	hardworking

Answer the following questions

1. Why was Mahindra's father worried?
2. Give reasons for:
   (a) Akshay's mother sold all her jewellery and household goods.
   (b) Savitri refused to accept Sanjay's offer of financial help.
3. How do you know that Savitri was a skilled craftswoman?
4. What kind of a person was Nityakali?
5. What pledge had Akshay taken? What prompted him to take this pledge?
6. "I am not entitled to this reward. I've done wrong."
   (a) Who said these words and when?
   (b) Who was actually entitled to the reward?
   (c) What wrong had the speaker done?
7. What did Manindra have to do to pay for Akshay's stipend?

Formative Questions

1. Activity in pairs - Discuss with your partner two things that your parents worry about the most.
2. Think of a situation when you received praise for doing something. You knew that you did not actually deserve it. What did you do? Record your thoughts in your diary.

The Nuisance

Summative Questions

1. Give reasons for:
   (a) Kiran was lonely and bored.
   (b) Sharat's whacks did not bother Nilkanta.
   (c) Nilkanta started behaving peculiarly.

2.   What did Kiran do when she heard that a Brahmin boy was in her garden?
3.   Write about two dishonest things that Nilkanta did.
4.   'They spent the days chasing each other'. Who are the two people involved here?
5.   What was Nilkanta accused of?

Formative Questions

1   Do you think Nilkanta was right in stealing the inkstand? Justify your answer.
2   Fill in the blanks with key words and phrases from the lesson.
     a) The bus collided with the car, but fortunately the passengers had a _____ _____ .
     b) Rebecca was so jealous of her friend that she went all out to _____ her name.

Wish Fulfilment

Summative Questions

Answer the following questions
1.   'A name does not reflect a person.' Give two examples from the text to justify this statement.
2.   What excuse did Sushil give for not wanting to go to school on a Saturday?
3.   "If I were as old as my father, I could do as I pleased and no one could look me up." Who said these words and in what context?

4. What troubles did Sushil and Subal face as a result of the transformation? Fill in the respective columns.

Sushil	Saibal

Formative Questions
1. Have you heard the saying "The grass is always greener on the other side"? What does it mean? Do you think it is applicable to this story? Give a reason for your answer.

The Runaway

Summative Questions
1. Write a few sentences about Tarapada.
2. Why couldn't Tarapada be tied down to his house?
3. "Let me sing this for you"- Who said there words? What did he sing? Who was the audience?
4. Why do you think Charushashi was jealous of Tarapada?
5. How did Tarapada try to win over Charushashi?
6. What was Tarapada's new-found interest?
7. Why do you think Charushashi behaved strangely with Tarapada?

8. "Before the ties of love and affection could encircle him completely, he was lost again on a rainy night and gone to the aloof world at large." Explain these lines.

Formative Questions

1. Think and write: Why do you think Charushashi was jealous of Tarapada?

2. Fill in the blanks with the appropriate keywords from the text:

    (a) I have known her since childhood, but she remains something of an_____ to me.

    (b) We _____ alongside the quay.

    (c) The _____ sinner made a full confession.

    (d) Aruna rejected his suggestion with _____ .

    (e) Our library makes books _____ to everyone.

Shiburam

Summative Questions

1. Are these sentences true or false? Correct and rewrite the false sentences.

    (a) A gentle autumn breeze was blowing when a dog appeared suddenly.

    (b) The animal wanted proper human education.

    (c) The friends founded a club called "Fox Defamation Society."

    (d) The fox was named Shiburam to differentiate him from the others.

(e)   Shiburam's first lesson was to stand on his forelegs.

(f)   Shiburam could not find any resemblance between humans and himself when he looked at the mirror.

(g)   Will Shiburam remain an outcaste forever or will he be accepted by his pack?

2.   *Reason out:*

(a)   Shiburam's face fell and his skin became dry.

(b)   The fox's aunt and other relatives were in tears.

Formative Questions

1.   Collective Nouns: 'Pack' and 'cluster' are collective nouns. Make a list of ten more collective nouns.

2.   In what other context would you use the word 'club-house'?

The Scientist

Summative Questions

How well have you understood the lesson? Answer the given questions and find out.

1.   Which character do you like best in this story and why?

2.   Make a list of things that Nilmoni Babu lost and where he found them. Give your answers in the respective columns.

Things he lost	Where they were found

Formative Questions
1.   Which word /words best suit(s) Nilu Babu. Tick the right answer.
      a.   1. Fickle 2. Absent-minded 3. Restless 4. Trusting
      b.   1. Tidy 2. Organised 3. Slovenly 4. Eccentric
2.   Which word/ words best suit Nilu Babu's wife? Circle the words.
      a. Fed up with him   b. Intelligent
      c. Utterly taken with his ways
      d. Sympathetic towards him
3.   Scientists are many a time known to be absent-minded. Find out the names of three such scientists. Narrate/ discuss in class any one instance of a scientist's absentmindedness.

The Invention of Shoes

Summative Questions
Match the words on your left with their meanings on the right:-
1.   Smears   beyond explanation
2.   Ponderous   a loose cloak or shawl
3.   Unintelligible   spreads with a greasy or sticky substance
4.   Mantle   slow and weighty; serious
Answer the following questions:
1.   How did the people feel at the kingdom of King Hobu in the beginning of the story?
2.   What was the king wondering about?

3. "All gave out various sounds individually and collectively." Who does 'all' refer to in this sentence?
4. "You will take your wages for nothing." Who said this and to whom? What do you understand by this sentence?
5. Why did the entire city disappear into clouds of dust?
6. What harm did the water-porters and water-carriers cause?
7. Who started the custom of wearing shoes and how did it begin?

Formative Questions
1. If you were to head a country, what would you do for the welfare of the people? Write down five actions you would take, in order of priority.
2. Group Work : Form groups of seven or eight students. Assign roles to each person—king, ministers, common man etc. Give your kingdom a name. Make a presentation through charts, a drama, or even a powerpoint presentation of how your city functions.

A 'Good' Man

Summative Questions
Find out the meanings of the following and write them beside the word/phrase:
1. All ears
2. Saga
Answer these questions:
1. Who, according to Grandpa, is a 'good' man?
2. Describe Panchkadi in three sentences.

3.   How did Panchkadi steal Grandpa's golden fountain pen?
4.   Why couldn't Grandpa accuse Panchkadi of stealing his pen although he could see it happening?
5.   What was the next thing that Panchkadi stole?
6.   What happened to Grandpa's copy of Browning's poems?

Formative Questions
1.   Pair activity :- Enact the story with your friend.
2.   In one or two sentences, write who according to you is a 'good man'.

Return of the Little Master

Summative Questions
Comprehension: Think and Write.
1.   Raicharan had two masters. Who were they?
2.   Describe two pranks which Raicharan had to play to please Anukul's baby?
3.   What damages did the flood cause?
4.   Explain with reference to the context: (Who said these words to whom and when?)
      (a)   He gave one piercing cry, "Master, Master, little Master!"
      (b)   "The baby wore gold ornaments."
      (c)   "Your Lordship."
      (d)   "Good God!" he exclaimed."What! Where is he?"
      (e)   "... let him at least have a small monthly pension."

Formative Questions

1. What do you think happened to Raicharan in the end? Give your view in two-three sentences.

2. Write about the first three things you would do if you were lost in a huge crowd.

3. Group Discussion: Do you think Raicharan was right in giving away his own son?